*There are many versions of this classic
tale. In the tradition of the storyteller,
each one is uniquely different.*

Library of Congress Cataloging-in-Publication Data

José, Eduard.
  [Simbad el marino.   English]
  Sinbad the sailor / illustration, Francesc Rovira ;
adaptation, Eduard José ; retold by Janet
Riehecky.
     p. cm. — (A Classic tale)
  Translation of: Simbad el marino.
  At head of title: From "The Arabian nights."
  Summary: A retelling of the adventurous
voyages that made Sinbad wealthy and famous.
  ISBN 0-89565-472-5
  [1. Fairy tales.   2. Folklore, Arab.]
I. Rovira, Francesc, ill.   II. Riehecky, Janet,
1953-   .   III. Sinbad the sailor.   IV. Title.
V. Series.
PZ8.J747Si 1988   398.2'8 — dc19 [E]   88-36872
                                    CIP AC

© 1988 Parramón Ediciones, S. A.
Printed in Spain by Sirven Gràfic, S. A.
© Alexander Publishers' Marketing
and The Child's World, Inc.: English
edition, 1988.
L.D.: B-41.155-88

FROM "THE ARABIAN NIGHTS"

Sinbad the Sailor

Illustration: Francesc Rovira
Adaptation: Eduard José

Retold by Janet Riehecky

The Child's World, Inc.

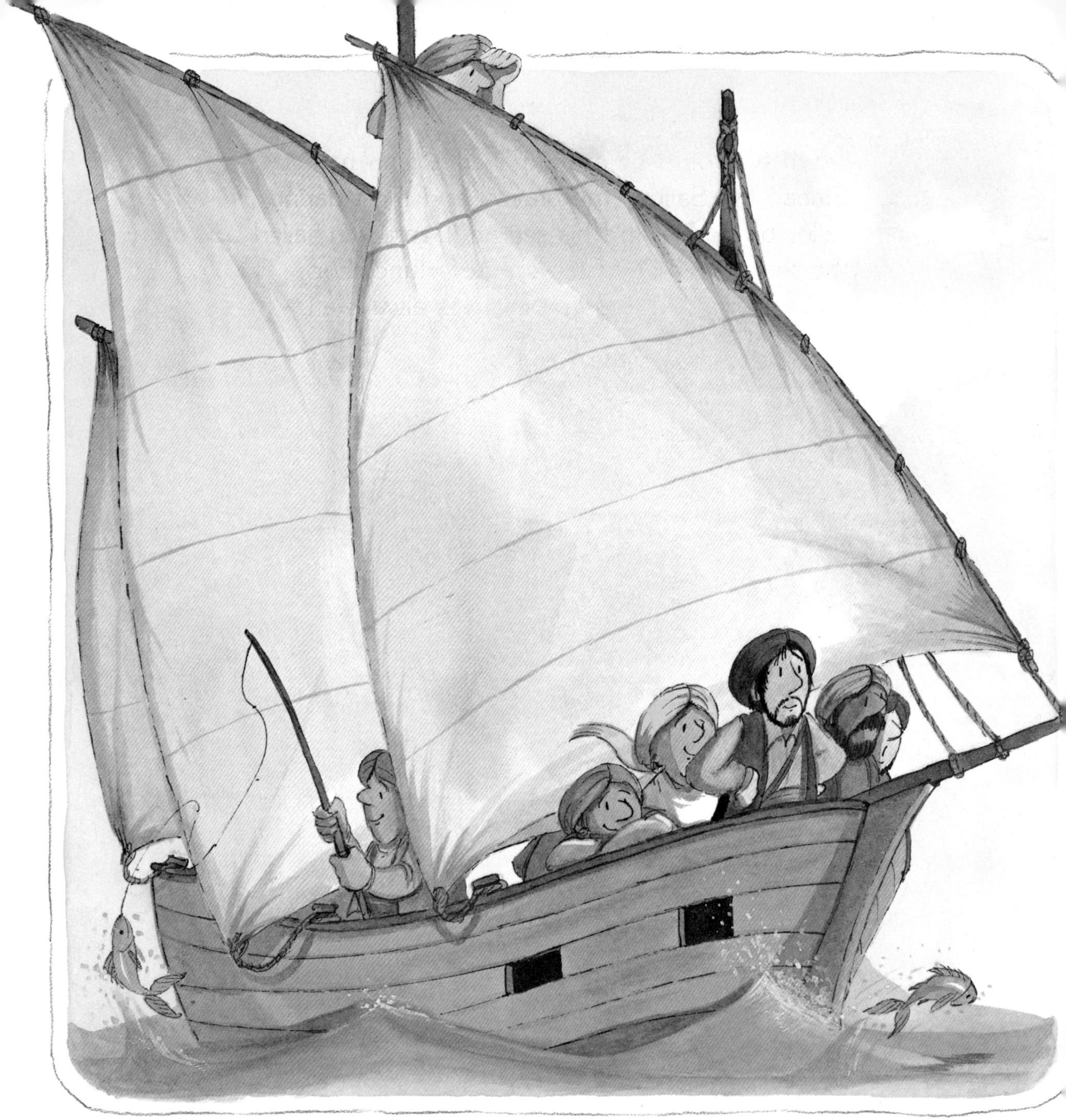

Once upon a time there lived a man named Sinbad the Sailor—the bravest and most daring sailor of all. He and his servant Benraddin sailed the seas in search of fame and fortune. For Sinbad and Benraddin, there was always an adventure just ahead. . . .

One bright, sunshiny morning, while afloat on their ship, Sinbad and his men searched the sea for a glimpse of land. They had been sailing for months, looking for treasure, but now they were lost.

"A strange rock ahead!" called the watchman from the top of the mast.

Sinbad rushed to the bow of his ship. He could see something in the water, but it wasn't a rock. As Sinbad and his men watched, a gigantic, green finger rose from the water. One finger became two, then a whole hand, and then a huge, horrible sea giant rose from the water.

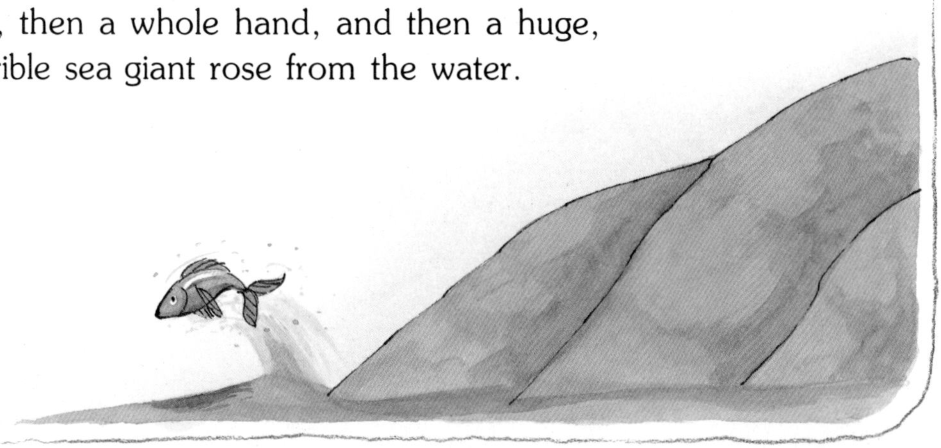

"Who dares to disturb my sleep?" thundered the giant.

The giant stooped and picked up Sinbad's ship as if it were a toy. He shook it, and several men fell into the sea.

"Let go of my ship!" Sinbad shouted, standing with his hands on his hips. "Why don't you fight with me, man to man!"

The giant just laughed. But because Sinbad had made him laugh, he decided to spare him and Benraddin—for a while anyway. The giant picked up the two little sailors in his huge hand and carried them to a nearby island.

"When I get hungry, I'll come back to look for you," he said, tossing Sinbad and Benraddin onto a pile of bones. Then away he went.

Benraddin trembled with fear. "These must be the bones from his other meals," he cried. "Oh, what can we do?"

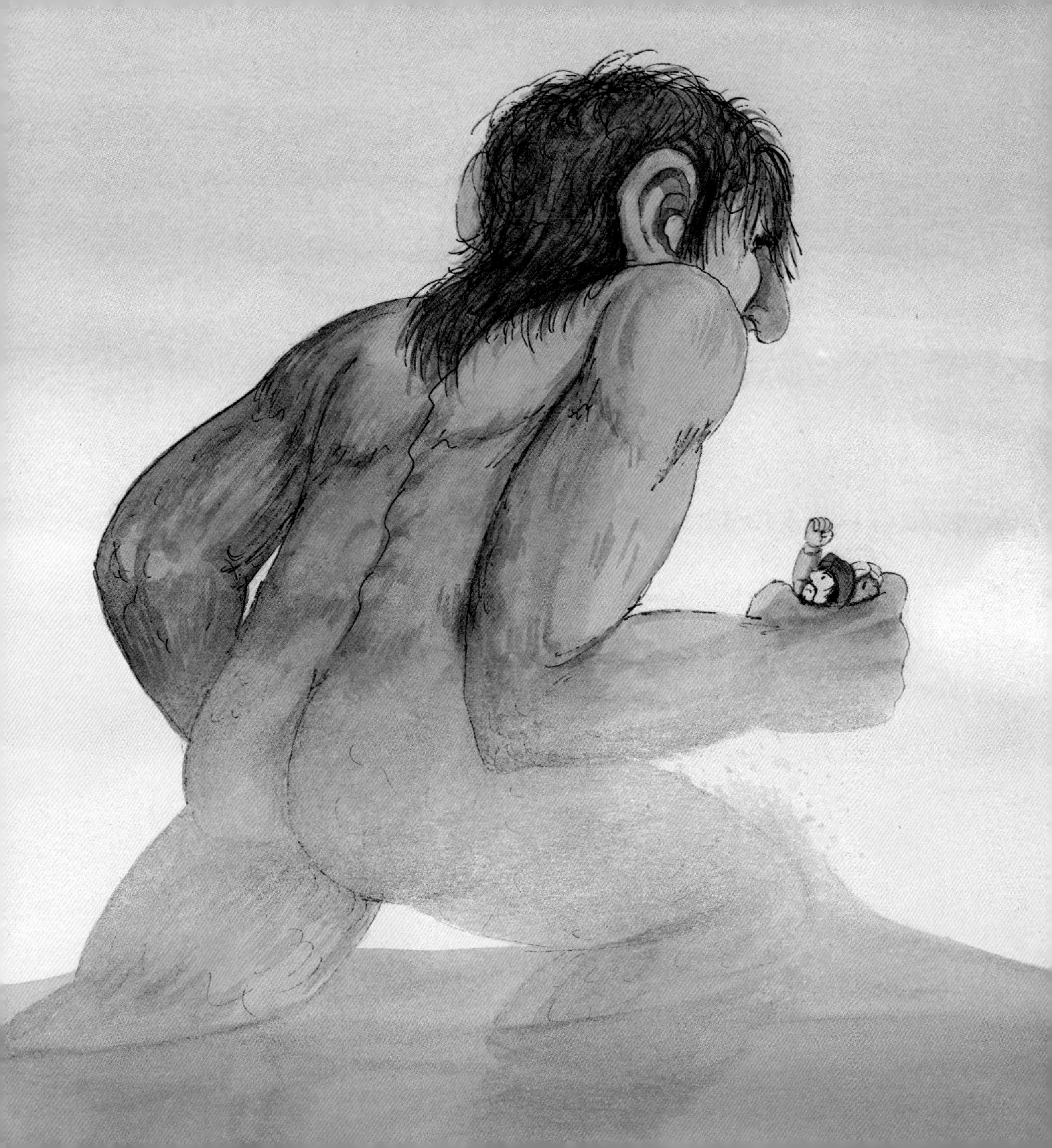

"We won't give up," replied Sinbad. "Help me with these tree trunks. We'll make a raft and escape."

The two sailors worked quickly. At any moment the giant might decide he was hungry! By the end of the afternoon, the raft was ready to sail.

Sinbad didn't care what direction they went as long as they got far away from that island. However, as the miles flowed by, he began to search the sea, looking for some sign of life. He was sure they had escaped the gaint, but that didn't mean they were safe yet.

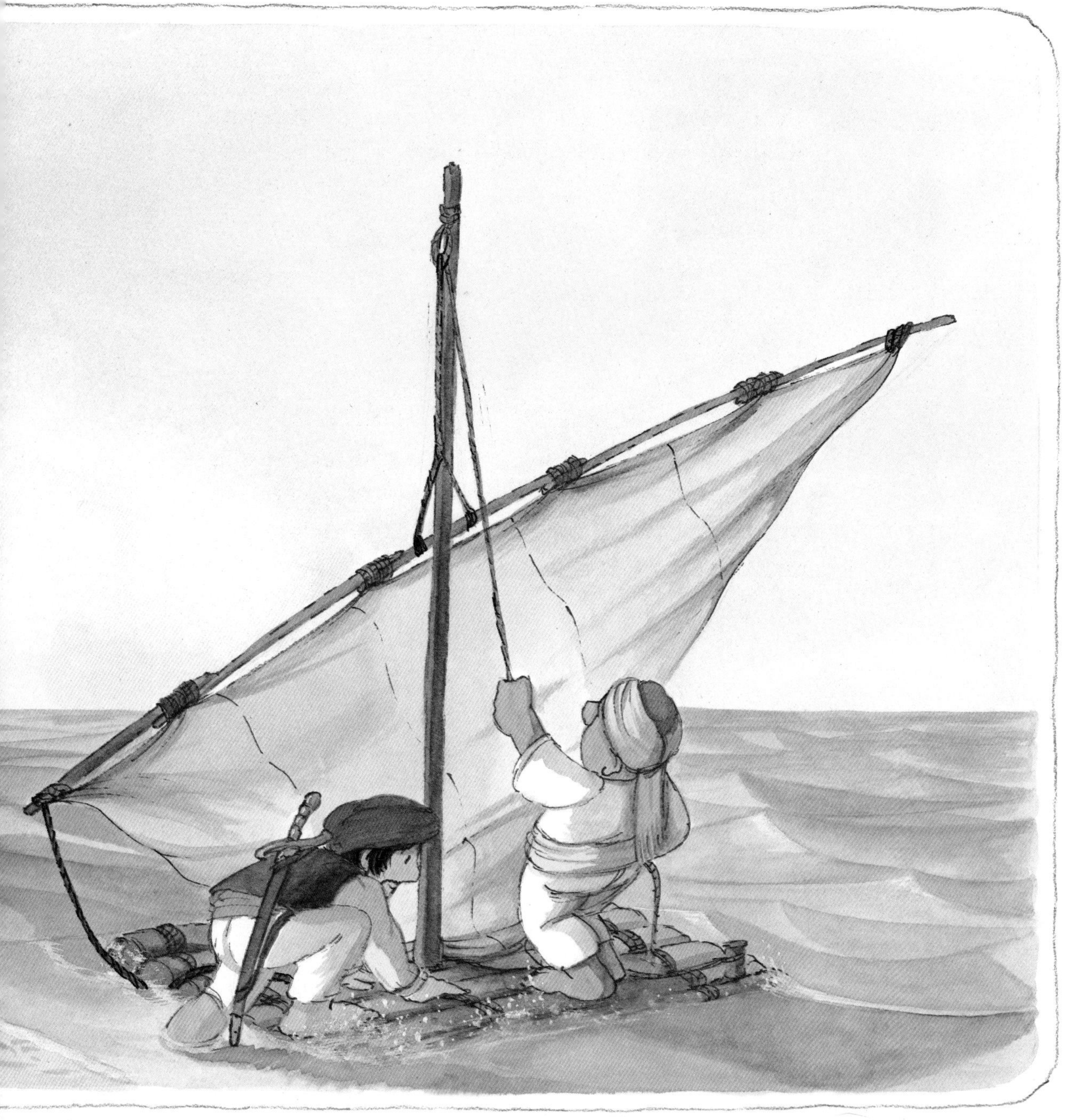

Night came and passed. The sun shone brightly in the sky. The two men grew hungry, and Benraddin began to complain.

"I'd give anything for something to eat!" he said. "Even a piece of a small bird . . ."

Just then the sky darkened as an enormous shadow blocked the sun.

"I asked for a small bird," Benraddin cried in terror, "not a monster!"

A bird as huge as a house flew over the sailors' heads. Its feathers were red and blue, and its head was like a giant eagle's.

"Wonderful," said the enormous bird. "I was just wishing for something to play with."

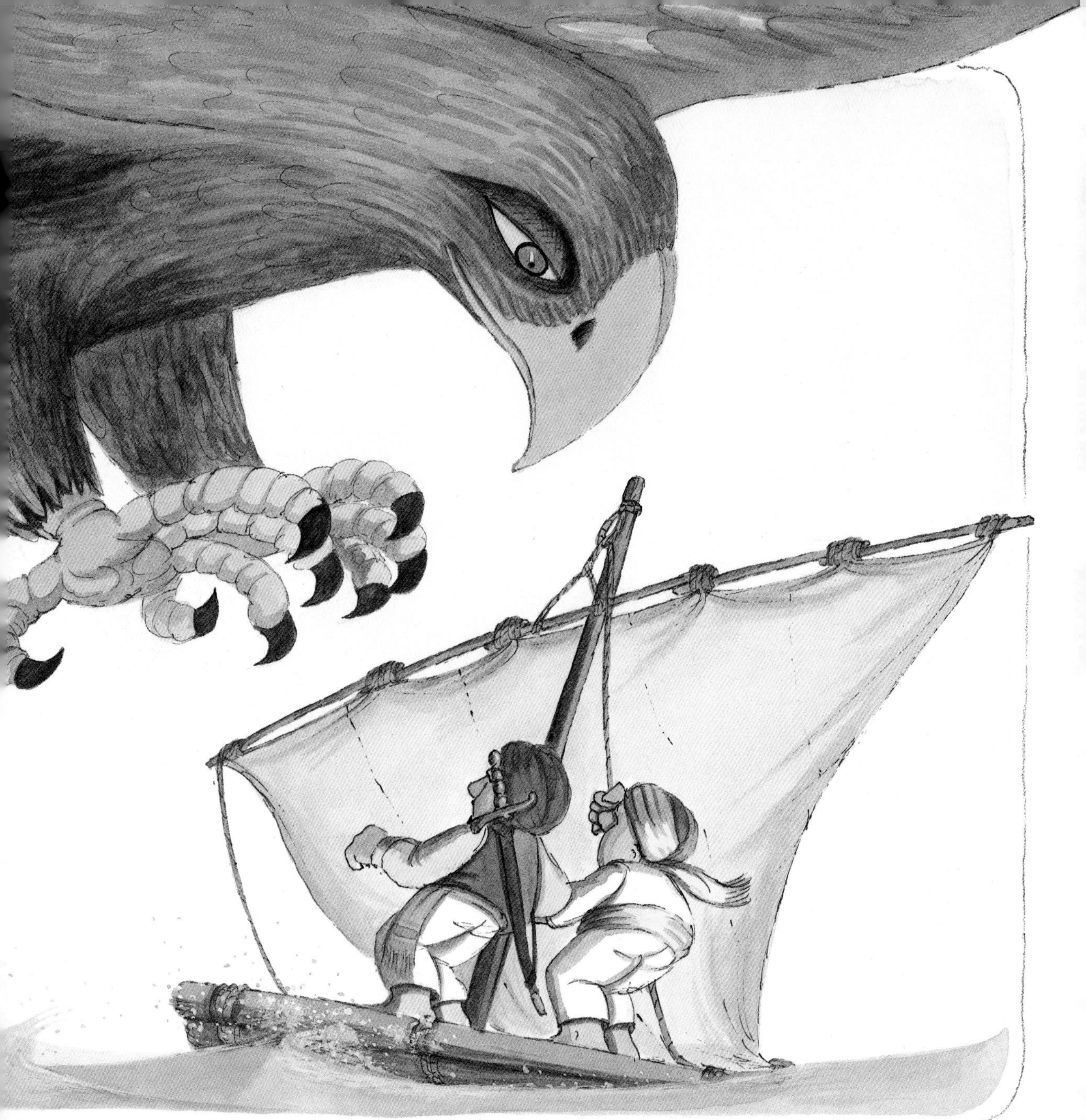

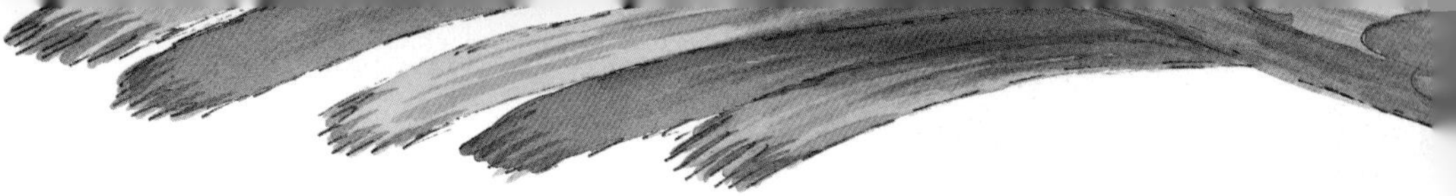

The bird swooped down and caught Sinbad and Benraddin in its claws. Then it flew high up into the clouds.

"Help!" screamed Benraddin. "I'm getting dizzy."

But Sinbad wasn't scared. "I have an idea," he said. "Just do as I do," he told Benraddin, "and we'll get away."

With that, Sinbad reached up and tickled the bird's legs. The bird started to laugh. It laughed harder and harder, until it lost control and opened its claws. Sinbad and Benraddin were free! Down, down they fell into the sea.

It was a long fall. And once in the water, only Sinbad's great skill kept them from drowning.

After some time, Benraddin cried out, "Look, I see land."

Sure enough, an island could be seen in the distance. Sinbad and Benraddin swam to the island and dropped onto the beach exhausted.

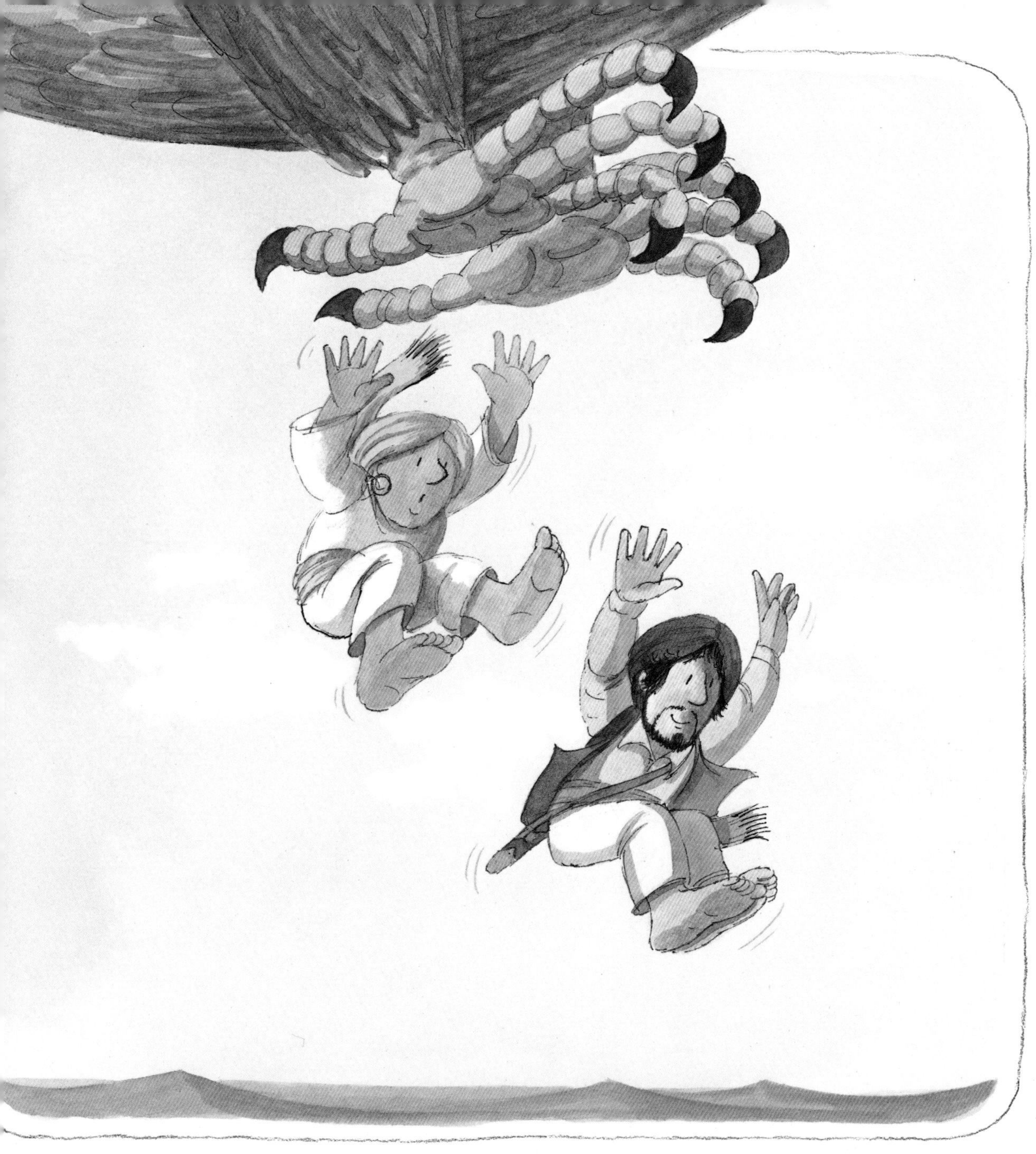

For a long time the two sailors lay on the beach without even opening their eyes. And when they finally did, they saw a strange sight. The whole island glittered with millions of bright lights.

"What can this be?" said Sinbad. He covered his eyes to keep the light from blinding him.

"Diamonds!" yelled Benraddin.

The light came from millions and millions of diamonds. The whole island was covered with them. They were bigger than even Benraddin could imagine. They were shining everywhere -- on the sand, on the treetops, in the bushes . . .

"What a waste!" said Benraddin. "We've found a fortune, but we can't use it. We don't even know where we are!"

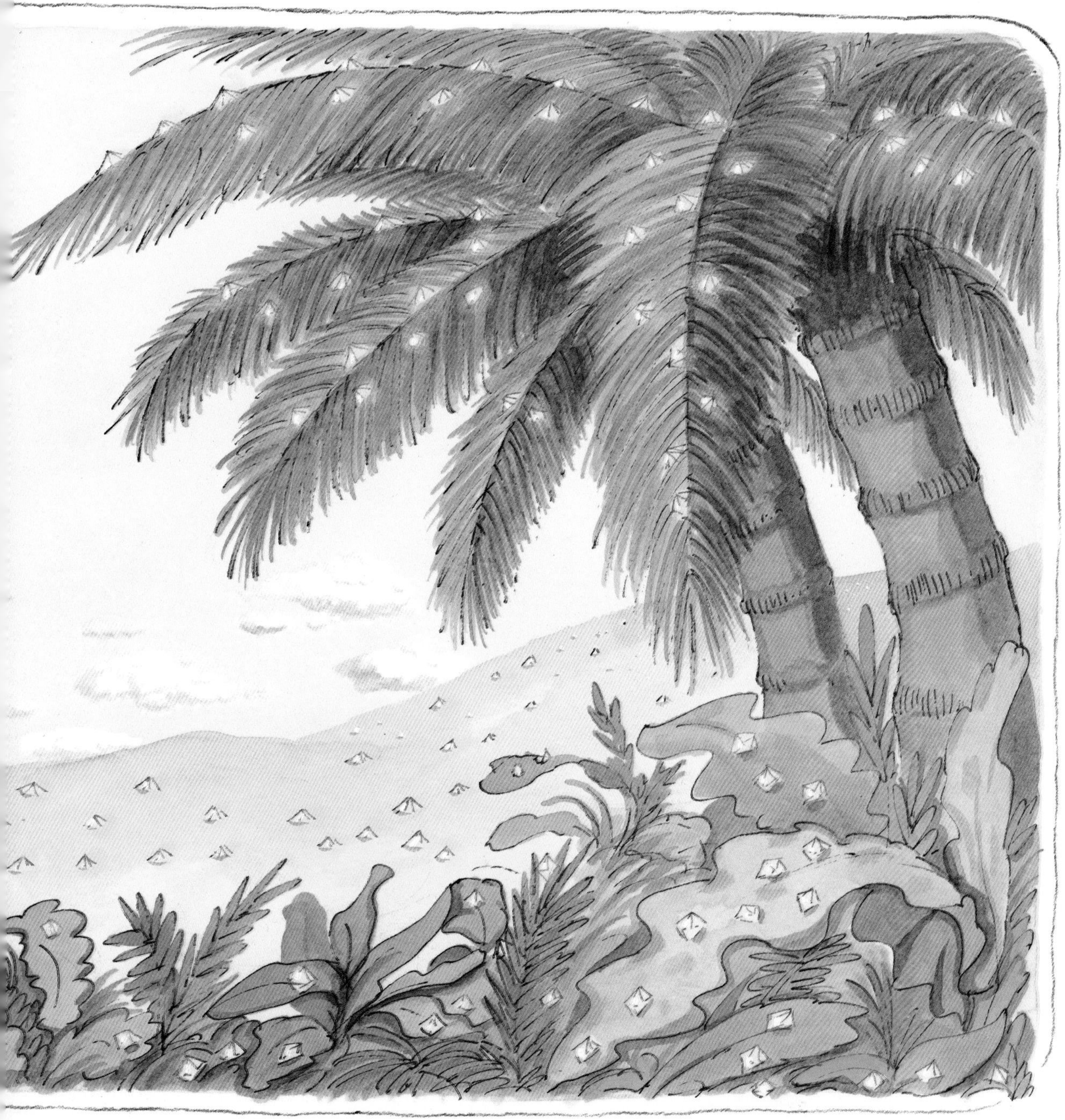

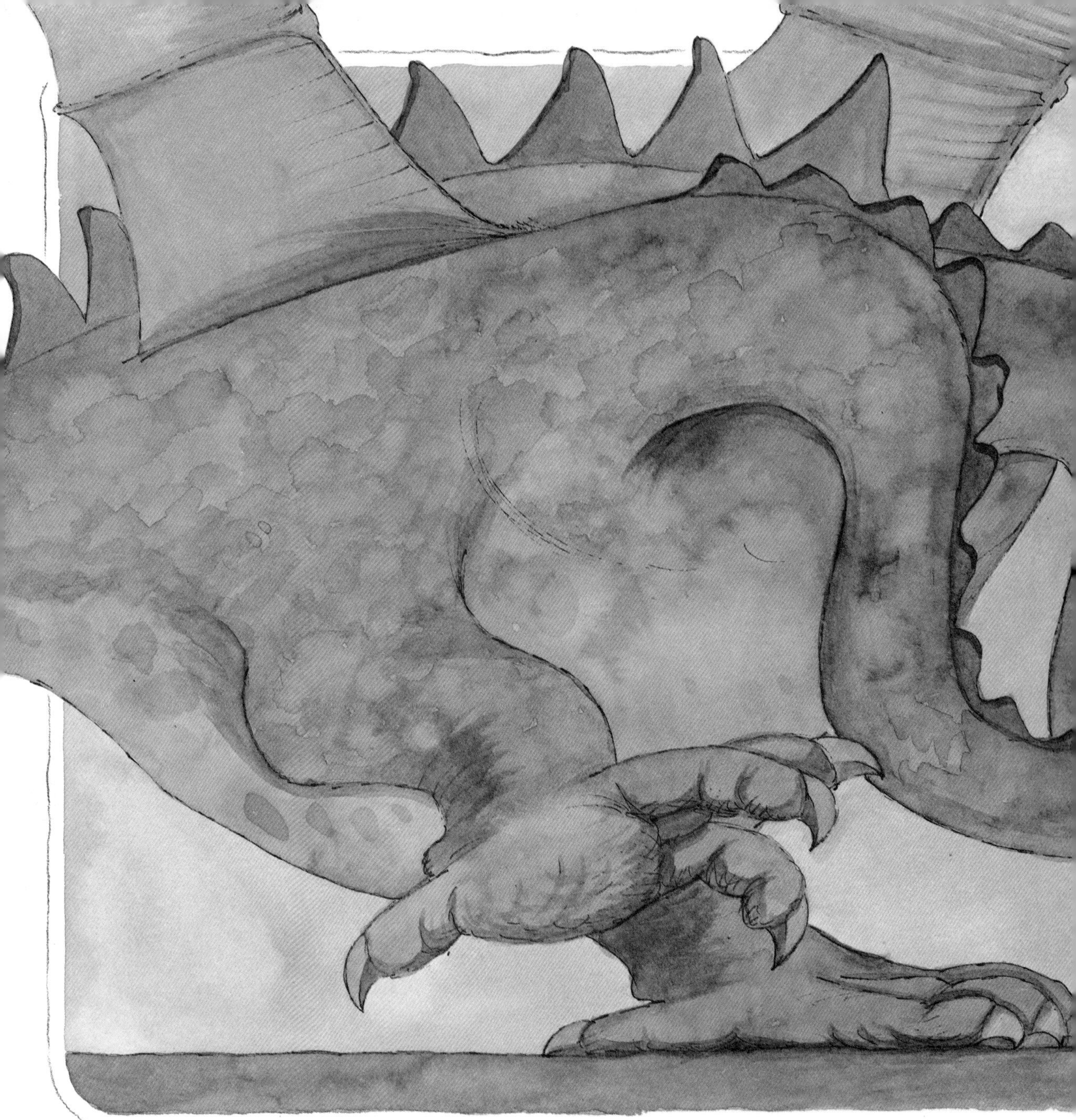

"I can tell you," boomed a frightening voice behind them. "You are on the island of the two-headed dragon!"

Sinbad and Benraddin spun around. A huge dragon towered above them. One of its heads reached for Sinbad. The other reached for Benraddin.

"Run, Benraddin!" cried Sinbad. "There's a cave over there."

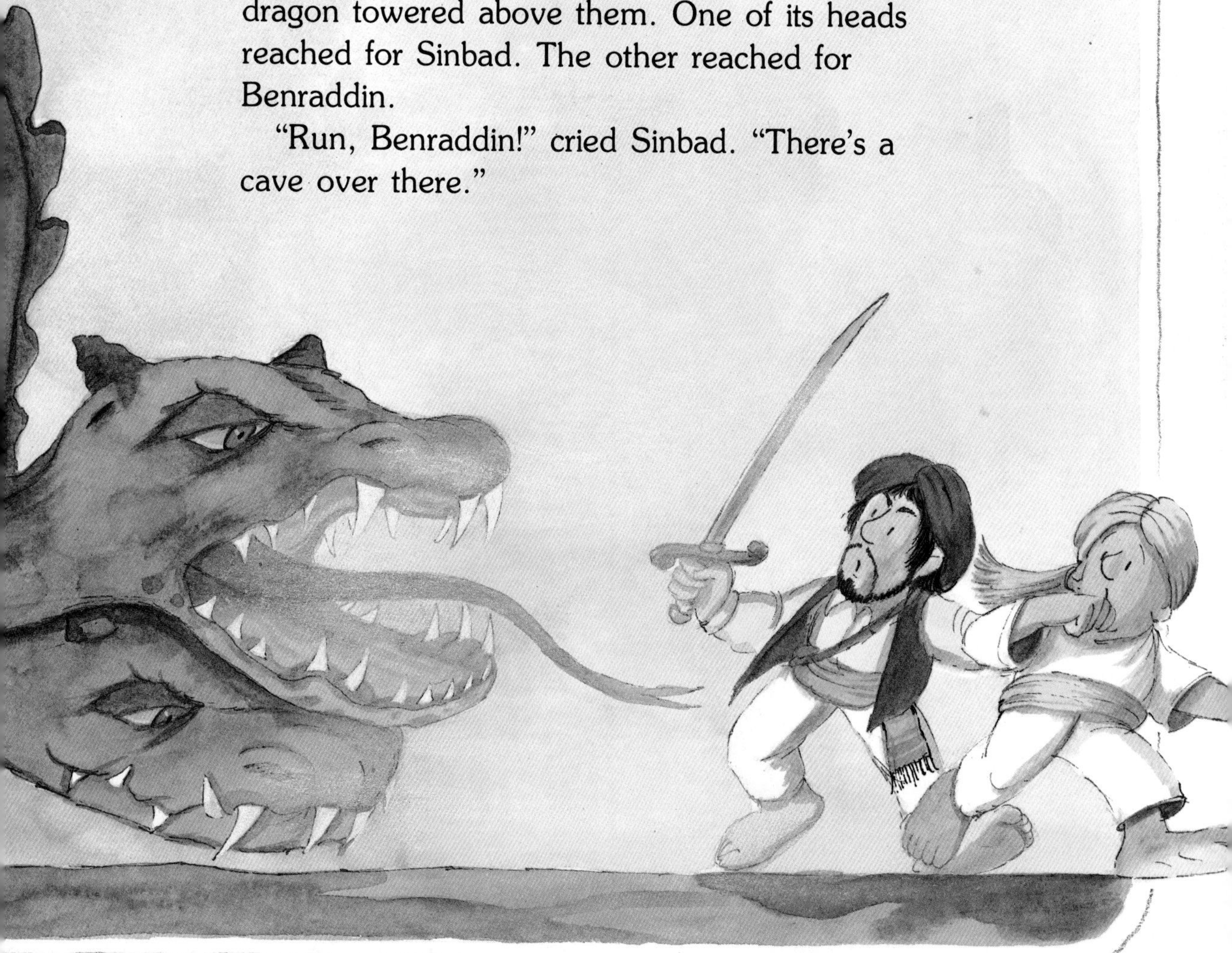

One of the dragon's tongues almost licked Benraddin's back, but the two sailors made it into the cave. Sinbad knew, though, that they still were not safe. The dragon could knock down the walls and chase them like mice. Sinbad searched for an escape.

"Look, a light!" he shouted. "Quickly, Benraddin. There must be an opening in the back of the cave."

The two sailors ran for the light. Once outside again, they could see the other side of the cave. The huge dragon was throwing balls of fire into the cave, unaware that they had escaped.

Silently, Sinbad and Benraddin made their way to the far side of the island. They had to avoid walking on the big diamonds that were everywhere. The diamonds' sharp edges could easily cut their feet.

"I'm so hungry," moaned Benraddin. "Right now, I'd give all the diamonds in the world for a good steak!"

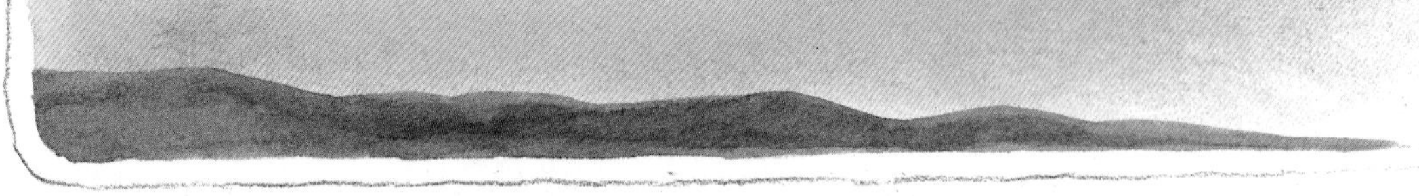

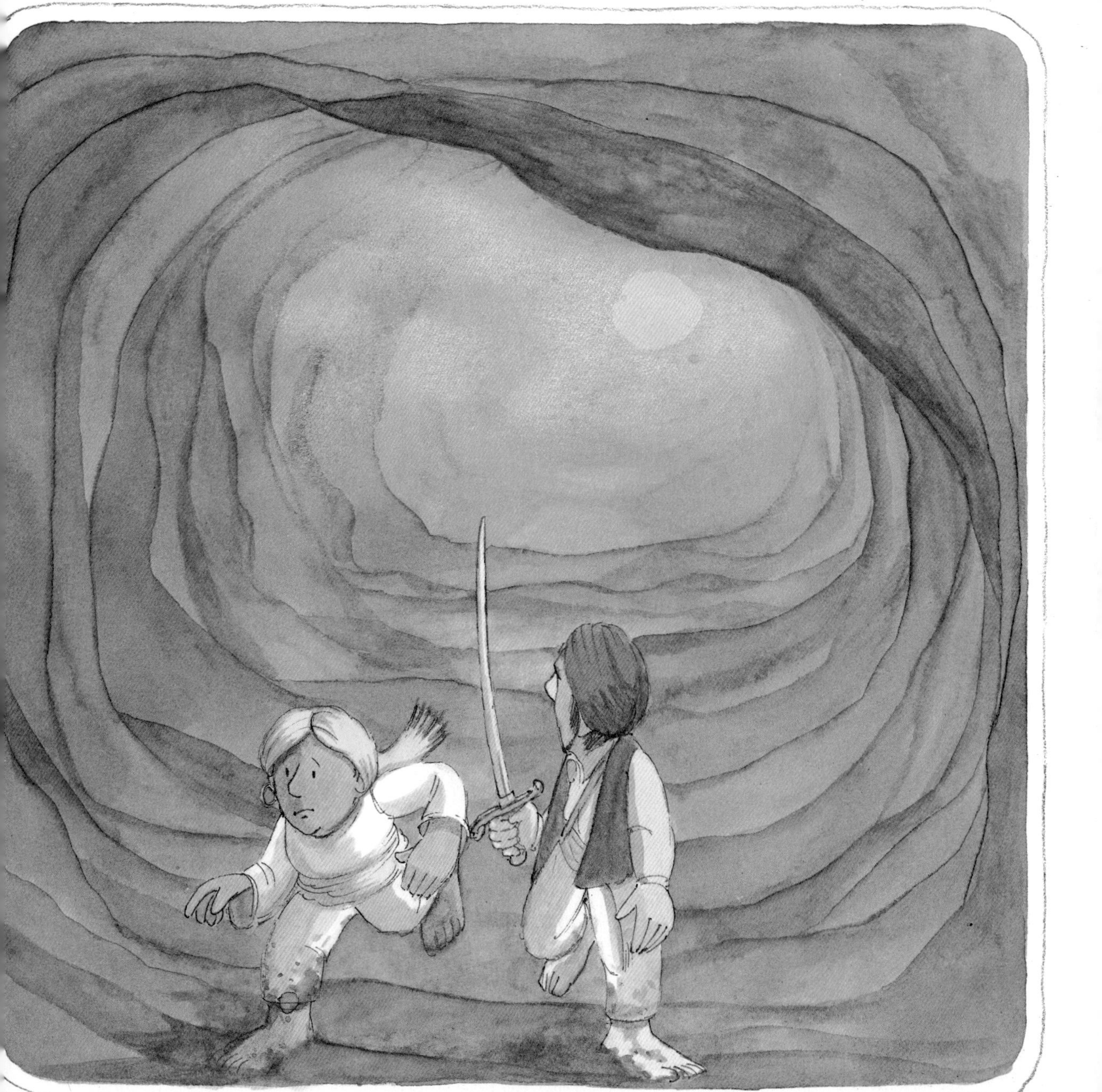

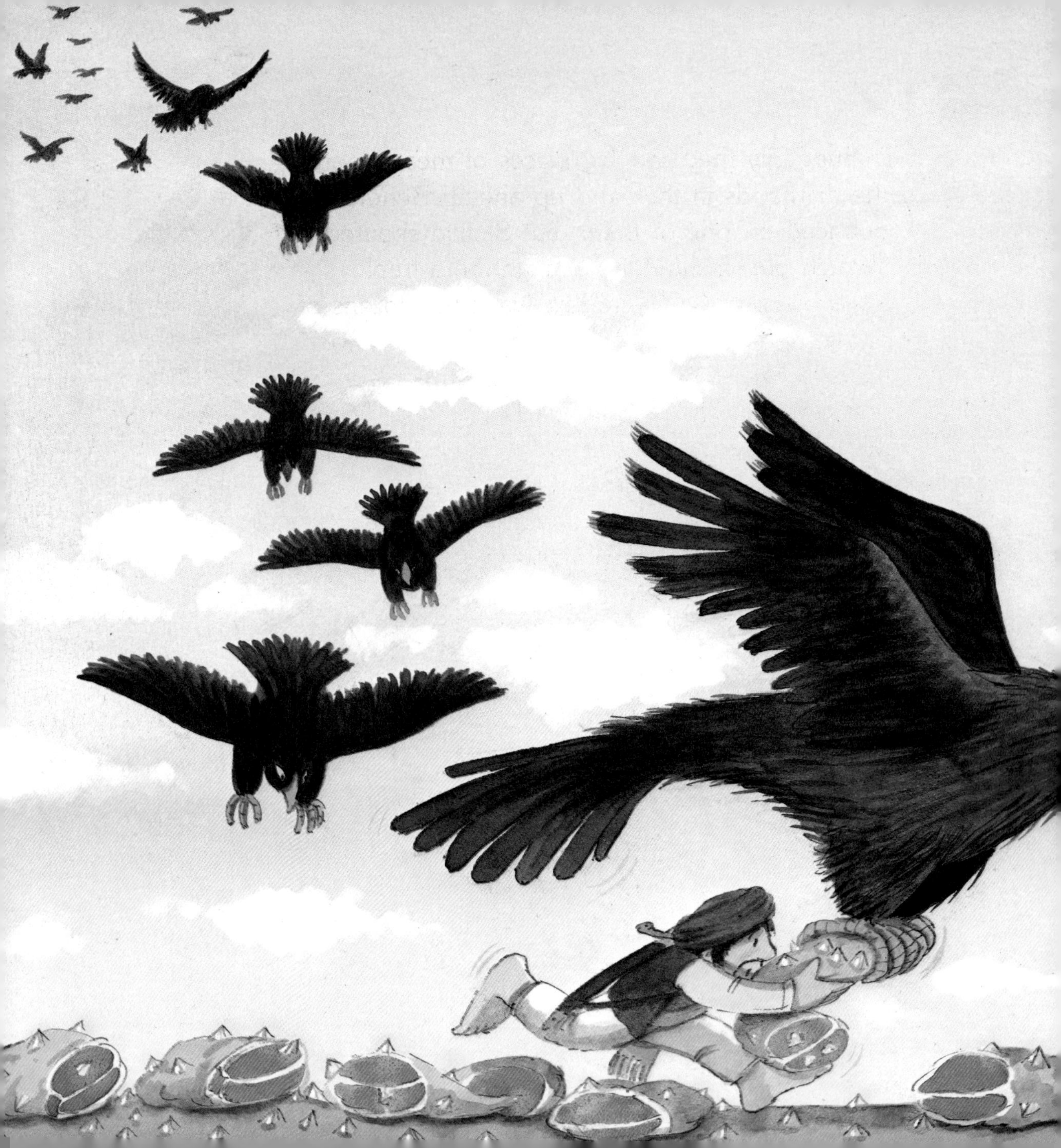

Suddenly they saw big pieces of meat among the diamonds in the sand up ahead. Benraddin pounced on one of them, but Sinbad shouted, "Watch out, Benraddin. It might be a trap!"

As Sinbad and Benraddin watched, dozens of eaglets swooped down from the sky. They were as big as elephants. Each grabbed a piece of meat and flew off with it. And, of course, each piece that was taken away had some diamonds sticking to it.

Sinbad got an idea. "Benraddin," he said, "hold onto a piece of meat. When a bird grabs it, go with it up into the sky."

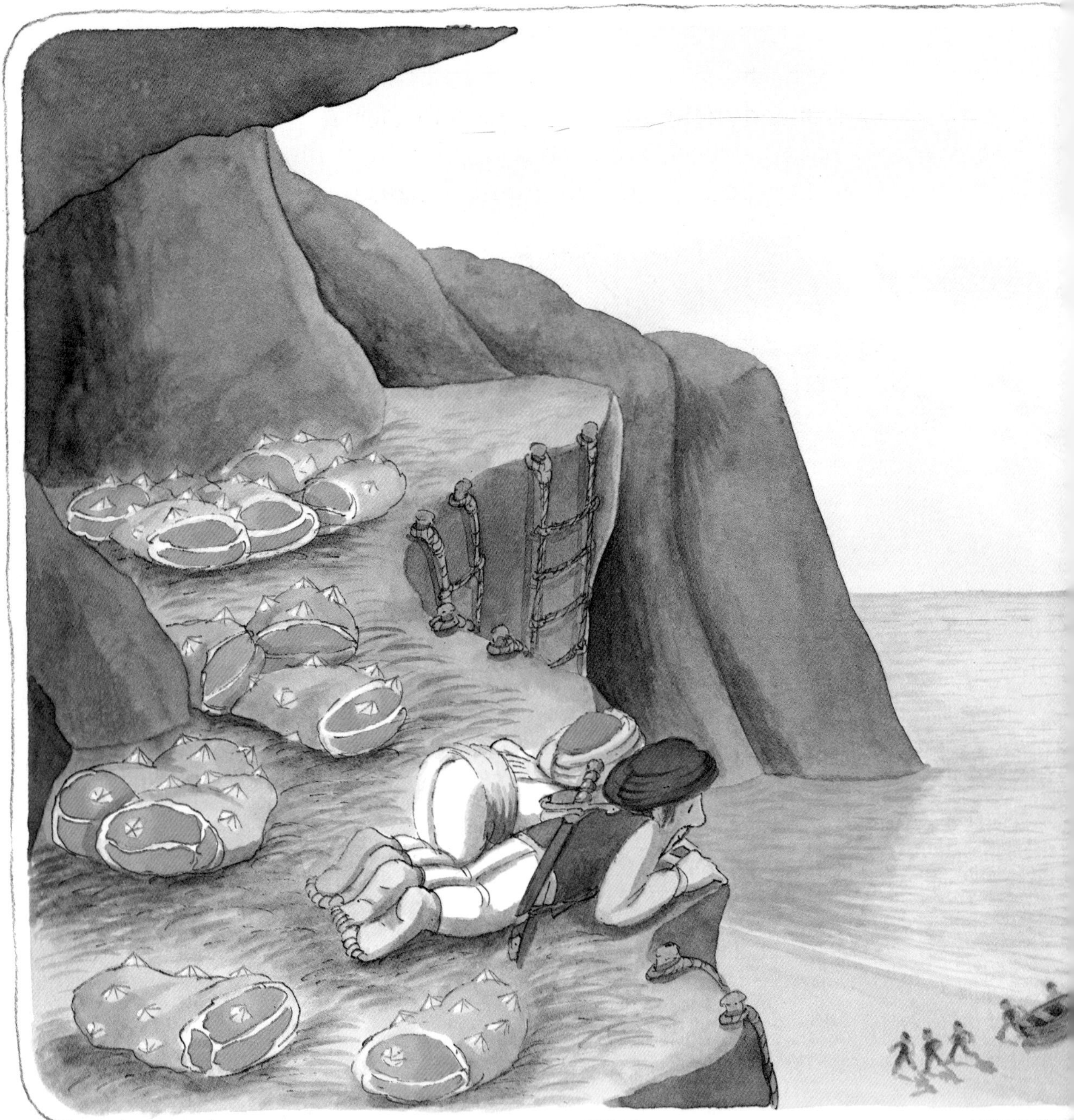

The two sailors did just that. Soon the birds dropped them with the meat into their nests. Sinbad noticed rope ladders going from the nests to the ground. And in a nearby bay, he saw a pirate ship!

"Aha!" said Sinbad. "This all begins to make sense. Those pirates are stealing the diamonds," he explained to Benraddin. "They throw the pieces of meat onto the diamonds. Then, when the eaglets take the meat to their nests, they carry the diamonds there too. The pirates can take the diamonds from the nests without having to face the dragon."

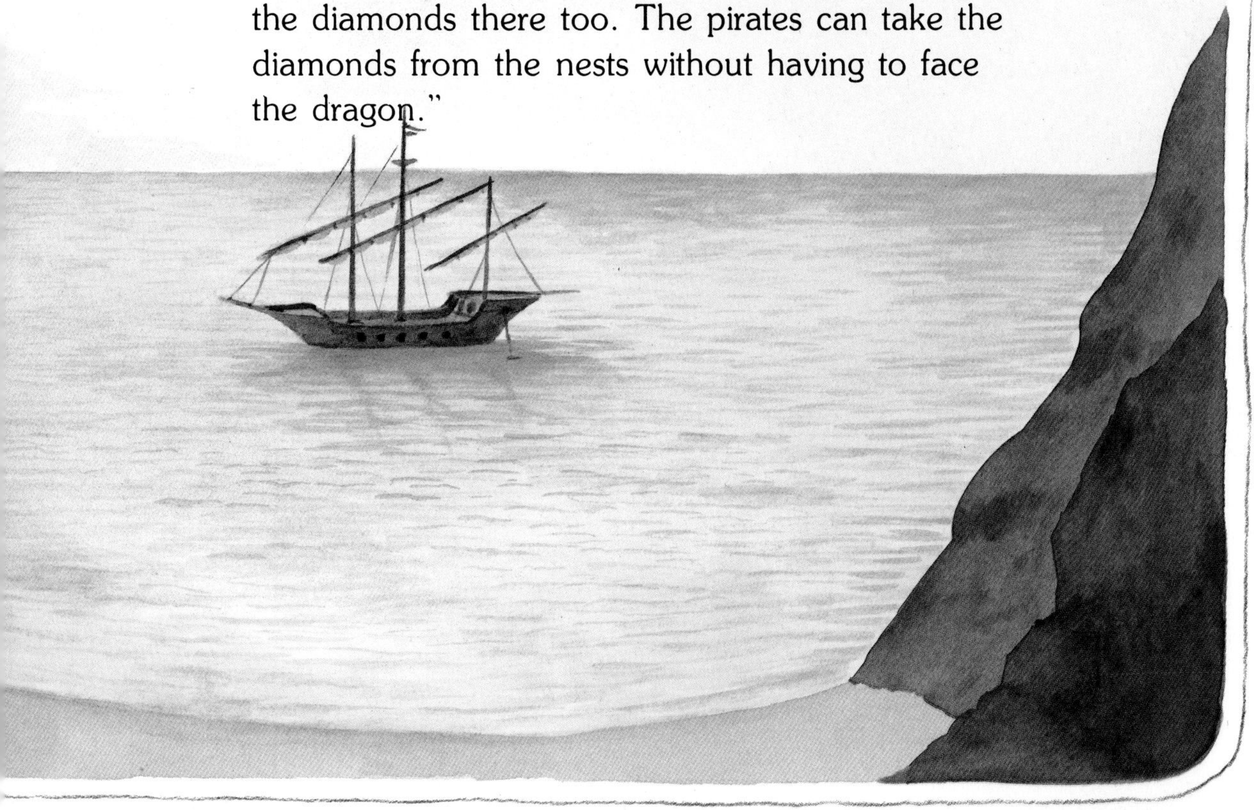

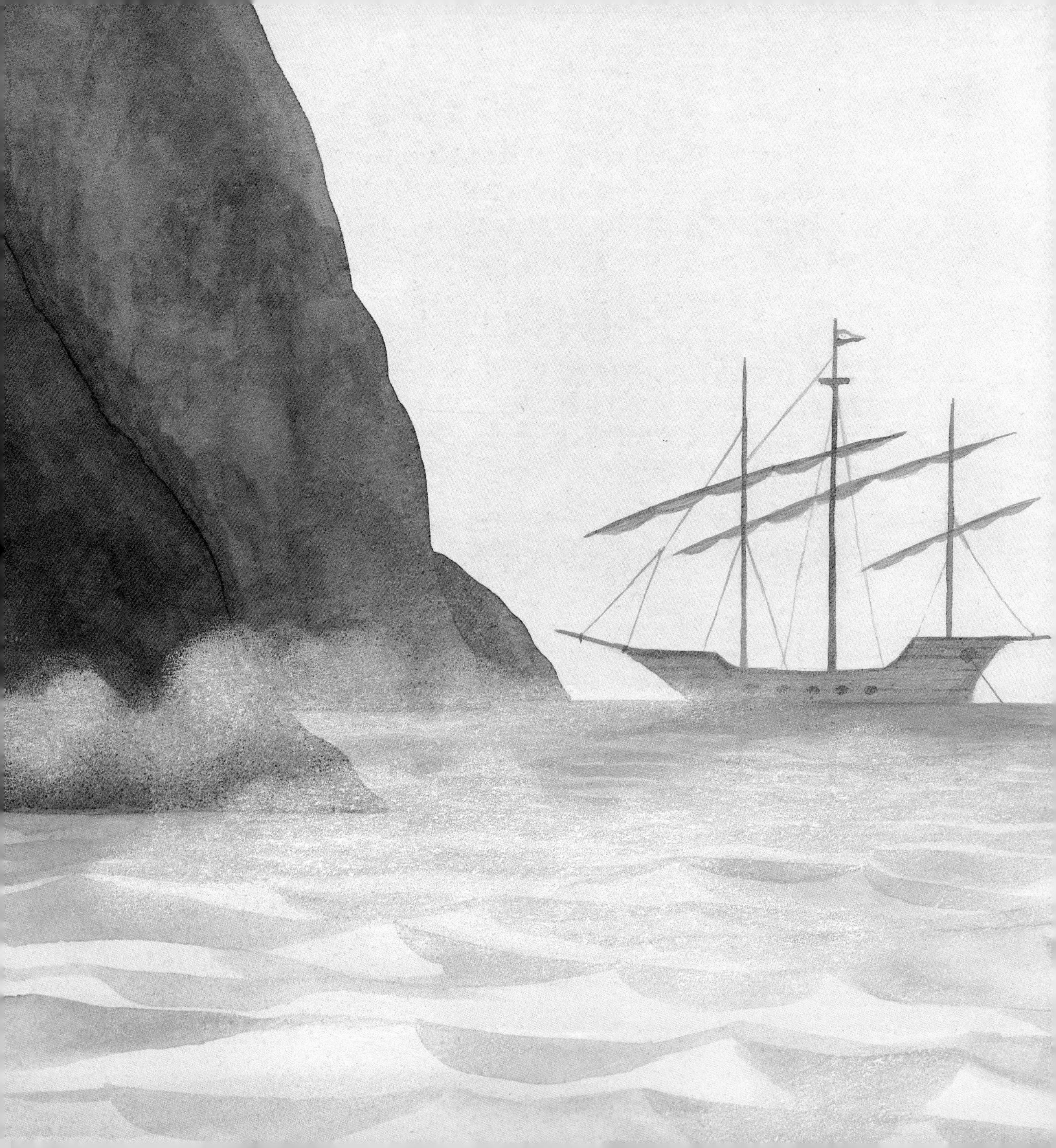

"That's all very well," said Benraddin. "But what are we going to do now?"

"We'll fill our pockets with diamonds and get away from here before the pirates arrive," replied Sinbad.

The two sailors filled their pockets and quickly slid down the rope ladders. Then they hid near the beach. While the pirates were busy collecting the diamonds, Sinbad and Benraddin stole their little boat and rowed off into the sea.

Benraddin was finally happy—not because of the diamonds, but because he had found a bag of food that the pirates had left on the boat.

"If we go with the wind, we might reach a friendly port," said Sinbad.

For ten days Sinbad and Benraddin followed the wind and the drift of the sea. Soon they ran out of food and drink. Benraddin almost gave up hope. Then, on the eleventh day, an exhausted Sinbad saw a well-known port in the distance.

"We're saved, Benraddin!" he cried.

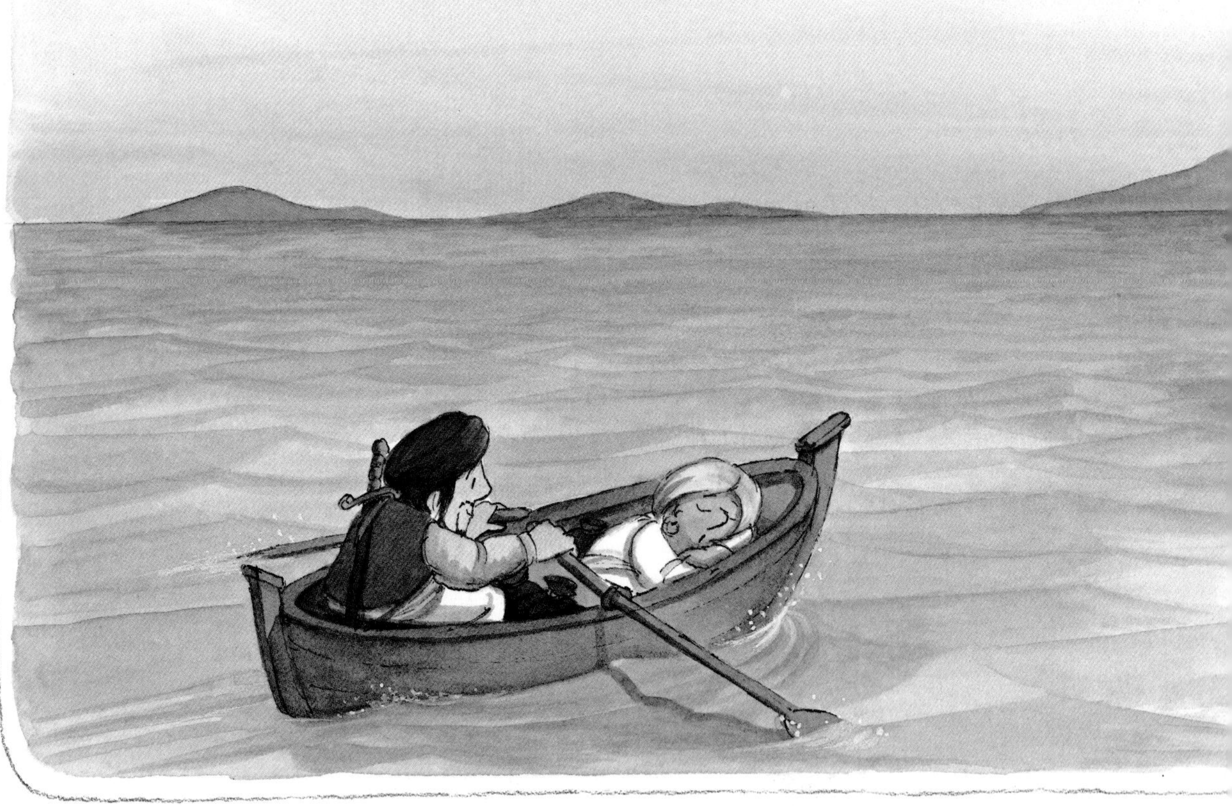

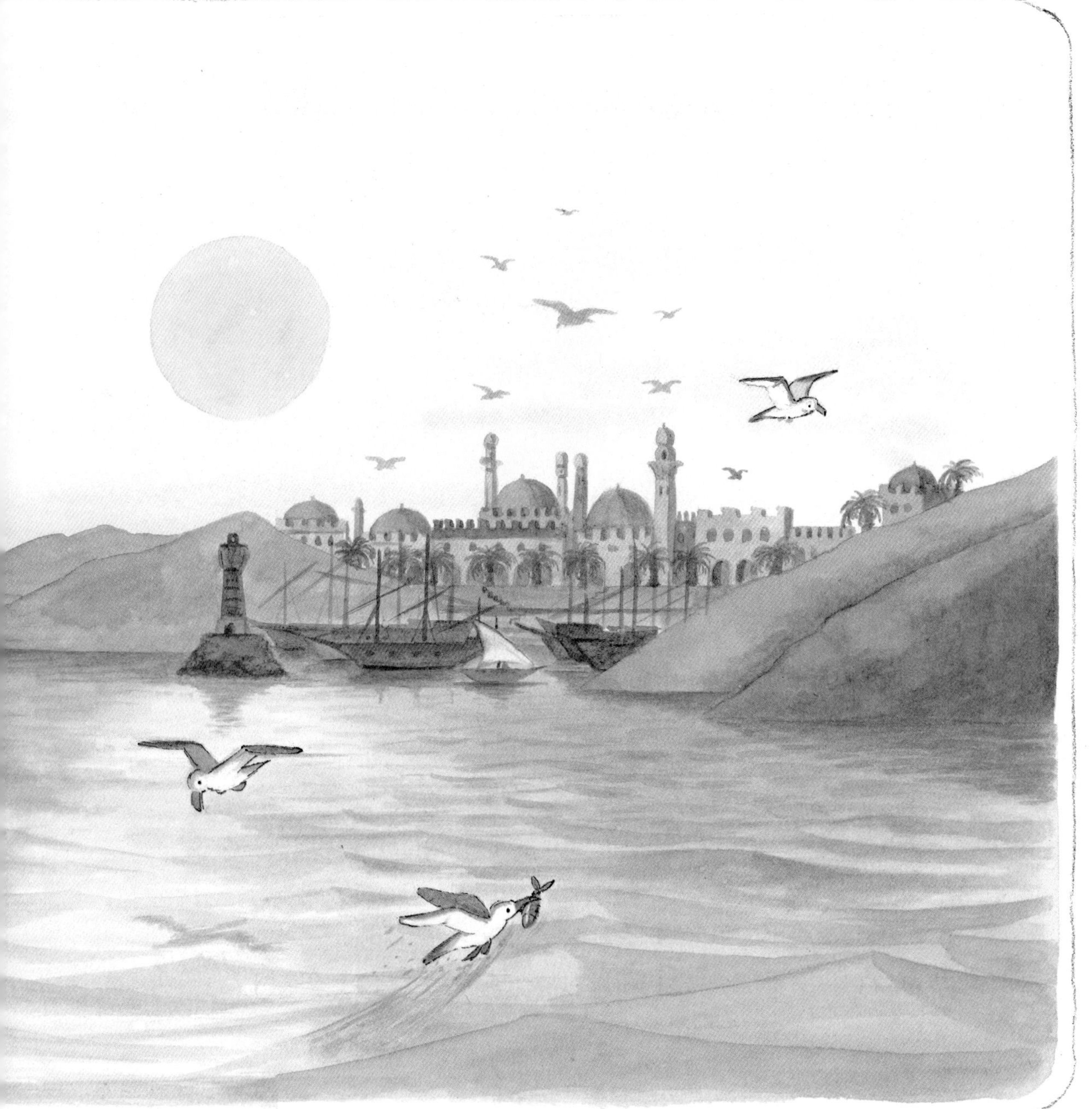

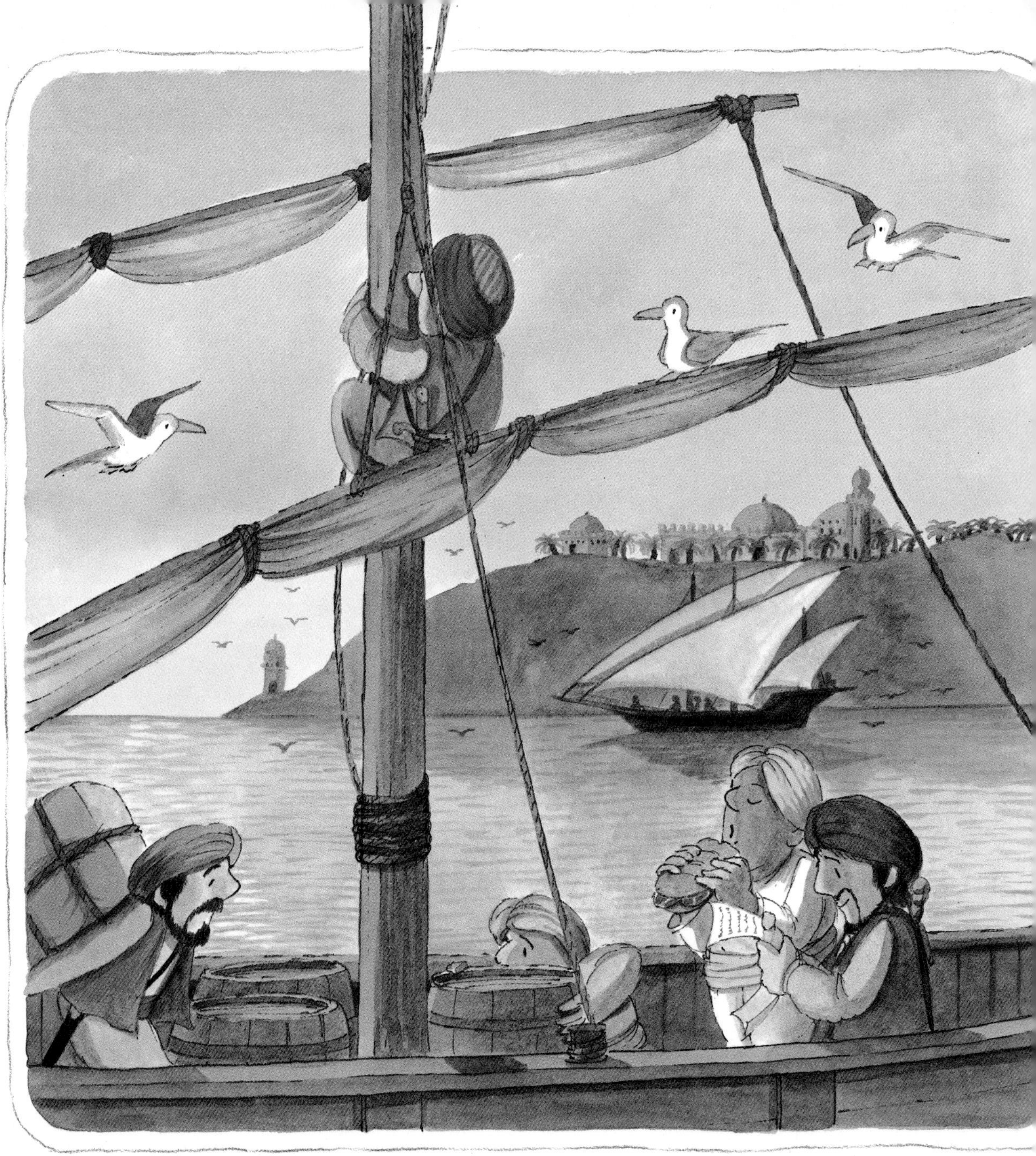

And so, Sinbad and Benraddin came to the end of their adventure. Not only were they saved, they were also very rich. The two sailors lived in the seaport for several months and recovered their strength. But they were not content to stay very long in one place. After all, Sinbad was the bravest and most daring sailor of all. He couldn't give up the sea! And so, one day, Sinbad and Benraddin decided to charter a ship and go in search of more diamonds.

For Sinbad and Benraddin, there would always be another adventure just ahead!